This book belongs to

www.makebelieveideas.com
Written and illustrated by Kate Toms.
Designed by Annie Simpson.

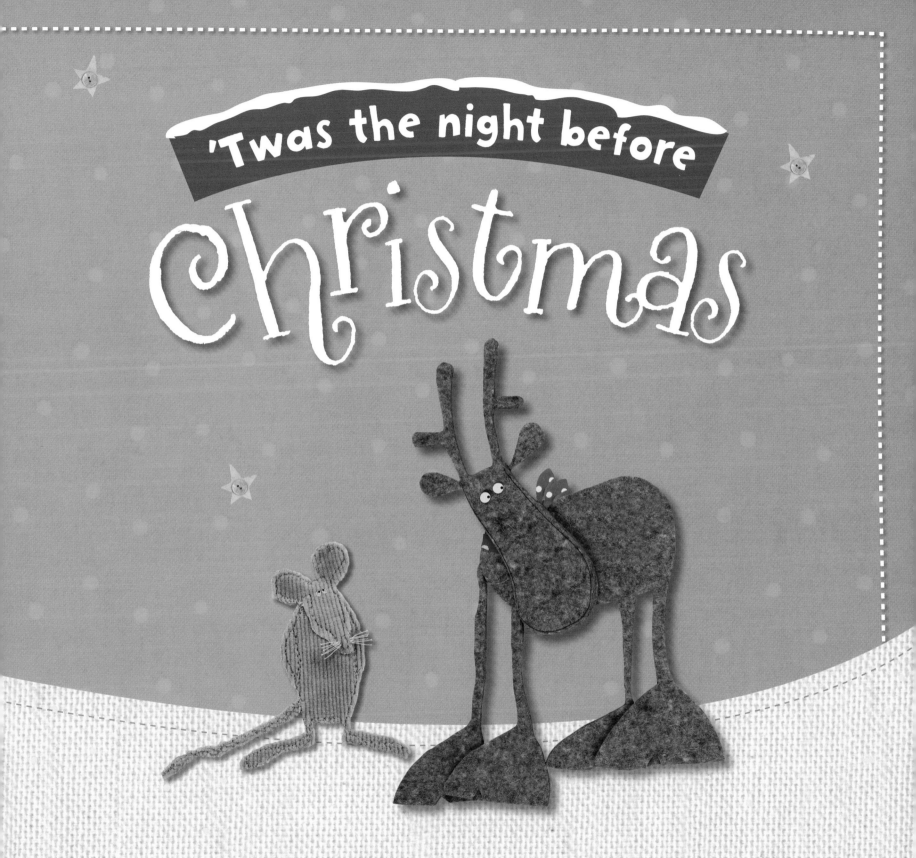

'Twas the night before Christmas

Kate Toms

'Twas the night before Christmas
and all through the house,
not a **creature** was stirring –
not even **a mouse.**

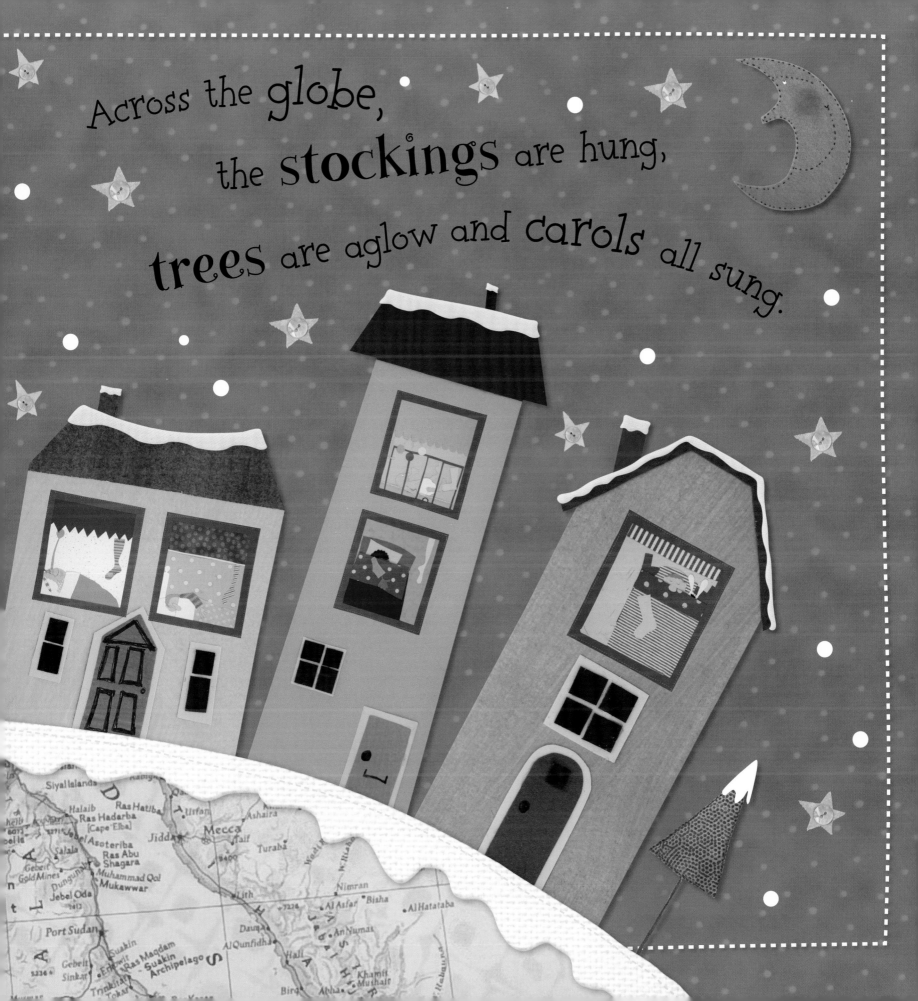

Across the globe,
    the **stockings** are hung,
trees are aglow and **carols** all sung.

'Twas the **night before** Christmas
and all through the *house*,
not a **creature** was stirring –
not **even**
a mouse!

Because Dasher and Dancer and Prancer
and Vixen and Comet and Cupid
and Donner and Blitzen
and Santa,
the pixies and
all of the elves,

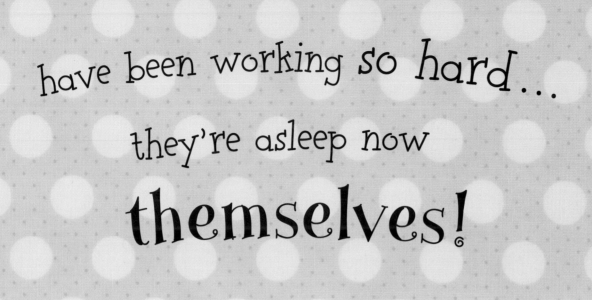

have been working so hard...

they're asleep now

themselves!

For weeks they've been cutting and sticking and sewing, warm in the workshop while outside it's snowing,

making the puzzles,
the dolls and the **toys** –
beautiful **presents** for **good** girls
and boys.

'Twas the **night before** Christmas and all through the **house**, not a **creature** was stirring –

except for a mouse.

He opens one eye and looks at the clock and seeing the time has a **terrible** shock!

Their afternoon nap has gone on **too long**.
It looks like Christmas could go
horribly wrong!

"Squuuueeeeeee"

shouts Mouse,
as he sounds
the alarm.

"eak!"

"Don't panic," says Santa, "Try to stay calm!"

He hitches the reindeer up to the sleigh and quick as a flash they're on their way.

GOOD BOY

GOOD GIRL

With a sigh of relief, Mouse waves goodbye as Santa's reindeer fly into the sky.

But looking around,
Mouse sees some **feet**,
underneath his favourite seat.
Curled up in a little **ball**
is the smallest reindeer of them all.

He wakes to find he's been left out
(he hadn't heard
the final shout) –

and letting out a little sigh,
he looks like he's about to cry.

"They've left you here," says Mouse. "It's true. But I've a **special** job for **you!** It's foggy, and they'll need a hand knowing where it's safe to land."

So Mouse and Reindeer set about laying lots of **candles** out.

Before long, Santa's flying back,
no presents in his empty sacks.

The **fog** is thick, but Santa sees
a runway **glowing** through the trees.

Santa lands the sleigh at last and runs across the frosty grass.

What about me?

With a **big hug**, Santa wants to say,

"**Well done, my deer,**

you saved the day."

"Merry Christmas," the reindeer shout,

and Santa blows the candles out.

'Twas the night
after
Christmas
and all through
the house,